After A While Crocodile

 Alexa's Diary

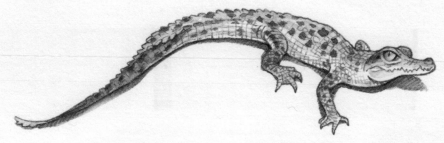

by Dr. Brady Barr and Jennifer Keats Curtis

illustrated by Susan Detwiler

with photographs by Brady Barr,
Jessica Rosnick, and Mario Aldecoa

This book is a fictional portrayal of a real program that allowed Costa Rican schoolchildren to raise American crocodiles in their classroom. This conservation and education project was designed for rural elementary school students who lived near rivers with a high potential for crocodile interaction.

April 5

From his baby pool, Jefe sees me. I named him Jefe because he seems to be in charge of the others. Jefe means "boss" in Spanish.

My little *cocodrilo* gazes up. He opens his mouth. *"Wanh. Wanh. Wanh."* He looks and sounds like a baby dinosaur.

Careful of his sharp teeth, I drop a piece of *pollo* (chicken). Jefe quickly lunges forward. My little reptile hungrily gulps the meat, swallowing it whole.

"Muy bien," I whisper to my crocodile.

the covered area where we go for recess when it rains

our school

our playground

our garden

American crocodile (baby)

spectacled caiman

American crocodile

spectacled caiman

April 9

I cannot wait to see Jefe. I caught a *ranita* (little frog) for him. In the wild, he and the other hatchlings would also eat *insectos* (bugs) and small fish.

In our *escuela* (school) in Costa Rica, we are lucky to raise American crocodiles. There are two kinds of crocs here—the American crocodile and the smaller spectacled caiman. The caiman gets its name because it looks like it is wearing spectacles, or eyeglasses. Unlike the caiman, the crocodile is a threatened species. We are protecting them. That way, hopefully, they will not become extinct like dinosaurs.

April 11

In the dry season, Dr. Brady Barr and another scientist rode *caballos* (horses) into the swamp along the long *rio* (river) to look for *huevos* (eggs).

Crocs lay their eggs in sand close to the water, but not too close, or they would get flooded. Caimans build mound nests that stick up from the land. Those are easy to find. Crocs dig holes in the sand, not something easy to find. In the swamp, Dr. Barr found a nest with 50 eggs in it. He only took 12, one for each of us. He left the rest of the eggs for the mother crocodile.

He carefully covered the eggs with moist soil and put them in a wooden crate so he could bring them to our school. We put them into the incubators we had built with boxes and light bulbs. The incubators help keep the eggs warm and safe.

crocodile nest

caiman nest

Crocodile eggs are white and shiny. They are about 8 cm (3 in.) long.

We waited 78 days for our babies to hatch!

Now, Dr. Barr and the rangers are teaching us about crocs and how to safely share water and land with them. I am glad that I get to headstart my *cocodrilo*. I will take care of Jefe until he can be released back to his river.

April 18

Some people think crocodiles are monsters. I know this isn't true. Not everyone likes crocs but we need them. They are a keystone species. In a building, a keystone is a big, important stone that holds all of the other stones in place. If you take away the keystone, the whole building could collapse.

Crocs are a keystone species. They help support the other living things in the ecosystem. Crocs dig burrows to escape the heat. Other animals, like turtles, sometimes share these underground caves. Little crocodiles are food for lots of animals. When they get big, crocodiles help keep other animals' numbers from getting too large by eating some of them.

Keystone of building arch

April 26

Crocodiles can make more noises than any other reptile. Jefe is noisy. He closes his mouth and grunts. He calls *"wanh, wanh, wanh"* when he is afraid. Sometimes he chirps. As he gets older and bigger, Jefe will learn to roar, growl, hiss, and bellow. Some big crocodiles sound like motorcycles.

snout

vent

tail

May 1

Jefe is growing fast! Today my *cocodrilo* measured 45 cm (17.7 inches) from snout to vent and 22 cm (8.7 inches) from vent to tail. The vent is where the tail starts. We take two measurements so that we know how long our crocodiles are with their tails and without their tails. Sometimes hungry birds, fish, and snakes bite off crocs' tails. Unlike many lizards, crocs' tails don't grow back.

I think about the crocodiles in the wild. Jefe has a better chance of survival because I take good care of him. In the swamps, croc eggs can become too wet from a flood so the eggs never hatch. *Mapaches* (raccoons), *lagartijas* (lizards), and *pizotes* (animals that look like raccoons with long noses and skinny tails) like to eat crocodile eggs and baby crocs.

May 25

Today, Jefe measured 50 cm (19.7 inches) from snout to vent and 25 cm (9.8 inches) from vent to tail. I fed him *insectos*. I still give him *pollo*, but I also try to feed him what he would eat in the wild.

It is hard to believe Jefe was only as big as a candy bar when he first came out of his *huevo*. I'm so glad I heard him cry "*wanh, wanh, wanh*" when it was time for him to hatch. Since his *mami* (mom) wasn't there to dig him out of the nest and gently crack open his egg with her jaws, he used the egg tooth on the top of his snout to push his way out.

June 3

I took a picture of Jefe's webbed feet today. He has five toes on his front feet but only four on the back. Before we let him go, we will tag him. A little metal clip will be placed in the webbing between his toes on the back foot. It's sort of like getting your ear pierced. It doesn't really hurt. That clip means the scientists can identify Jefe. If he's recaptured, they can determine how much he has grown.

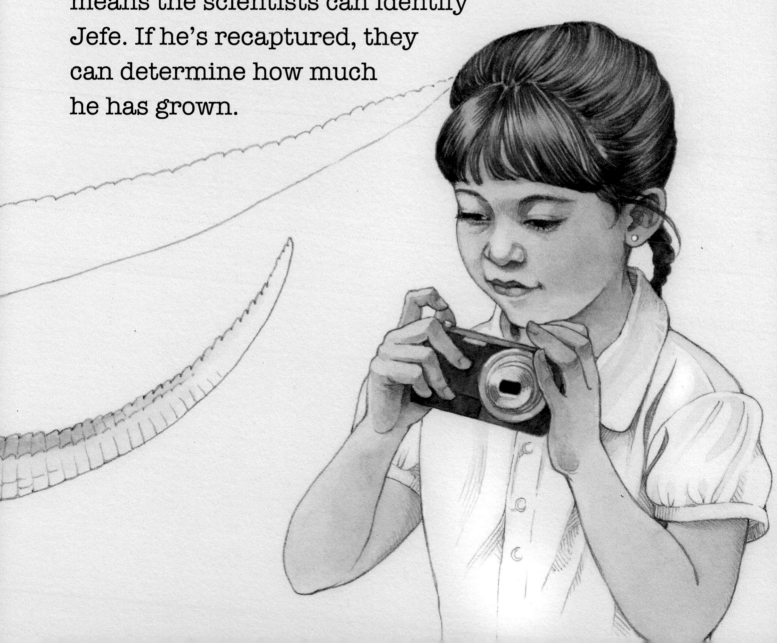

June 9

It is hot and Jefe is moving around a lot. He is cold-blooded. To warm up, he lies in the sun. The warmer he is, the more he moves around! To cool down, Jefe goes into the water or the shade, or he opens his mouth.

June 13

In just a few days, it will be time for Jefe to go back to his *rio*. He is as big as a loaf of bread and ready to take care of himself. I will miss him.

June 17

Today, Jefe goes home. I carefully carry him down to the river, holding him by his neck and just behind his back legs. I gently put him down on the ground. With a side-to-side motion, he quickly belly-slides toward the water. He turns around, as if to look at me, then hisses. I may have taken care of him but Jefe reminds me one last time: he is definitely the boss.

Adiós, Jefe.

For Creative Minds

Croco-what?

Crocodiles, alligators, and caiman are all called crocodilians. Crocodilian means different types of crocs. Crocodilians belong to three groups, called families. The crocodilian families are made of different species. There are 24 crocodilian species in all.

The crocodilian families are:

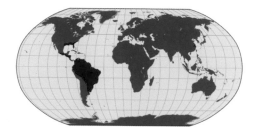

Alligatoridae
all alligators and caiman
8 species

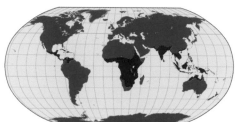

Crocodylidae
true crocodiles
15 species

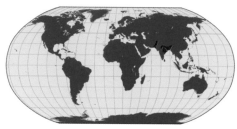

Gavialidae
the Gharial
1 species

How can you tell the families apart? Check out their snouts (noses) and teeth.

Snouts

Alligators and caiman have rounded snouts, like a duck's bill. The alligator's wide snout is better suited for catching and holding large, strong animals. A crocodile has a narrower, pointed nose. That's how you can tell them apart!

The crocodile's narrow snout is designed to quickly move side to side in the water to catch and eat fish. The longest, most narrow snout of all belongs to the Indian Gharial.

If you were a crocodile, which family would you be in? Do you have a pointed nose or a more rounded nose?

Teeth

You can also tell gators and crocs apart by looking at their teeth. When alligators' mouths are closed, they only show their upper teeth. When crocodiles' mouths are closed, they show upper and lower teeth, and a lot of them. Whether croc or gator, these teeth are attached to the most powerful jaws on the planet. You combine needle-sharp teeth with strong jaws and you have something like a bear trap. Yikes, you don't want to get caught in that!

Chompers

Whether they have a narrow or wide snout, the crocodilians' most important body part is their chompers (their teeth)! They need their teeth to catch food. The teeth are so important that they are constantly replaced so that these animals are never without a fresh, sharp set.

Sharks constantly replace their teeth, too. Rows of new teeth always move forward. Crocs' new teeth aren't like that. New teeth for crocs move up from below the old ones. Croc teeth are hollow. They stack up underneath each other, just like you could stack plastic cups. These teeth are hollow but don't be fooled. They are strong and needle-sharp! They aren't designed for chewing, like your teeth, but for holding on tight. Crocs don't chew their food. They swallow it whole or tear it into pieces that they can swallow.

There are big differences between your teeth and crocodilians' teeth. You only have two sets of teeth (baby and adult). Crocs will go through hundreds of teeth over their lifetime. Also, your teeth are designed for chewing. They match up so that the top teeth align with the bottom teeth. A croc's teeth don't match up. They alternate top, bottom, top, bottom, and so forth. They also are needle-sharp, designed for holding on tight. Scientists have measured the bite force of crocs at over 1.5 tons. That's the same weight as a small car. A person's bite force is 100 pounds. That's the same weight as two bicycles.

	Kid	American crocodile
mouth closed	no teeth visible	lots of teeth visible
teeth alignment	match up top-to-bottom	teeth alternate
teeth used for	chewing	holding and tearing
bite force	50-100 lbs.	more than 3,000 lbs.
tooth structure	solid	hollow
number of teeth in set	32	68
sets of teeth	2 (baby and adult)	unlimited

Dr. Brady Barr

I've worked on crocodilians for over 25 years, and have captured over 5,000, but I remember the first time I saw one in the wild like it was yesterday!

It happened over 30 years ago and I am lucky to be here to tell the story. I'd just moved to Florida, and being a lover of animals, especially reptiles, I headed to the Everglades. Before long, I came to a stream that came out of the woods and flowed under the road. I'd just started looking around when I spied him . . . my first wild alligator. I was expecting something big and ferocious, but what I saw was a tiny baby by himself. He looked like he was smiling at me! He was only as big as a candy bar. I thought he was beautiful with his big eyes and yellow stripes. It was hard to believe this little guy could grow to be 14 feet long. He looked at me and started to talk: "*Wanh. Wanh. Wanh.*" I smiled as I wondered what he was trying to say. Then I heard a huge noise, like a train rushing in fast. I backed up, not sure I wanted to meet what was charging through the brush. Suddenly, a huge gator came into view, racing right toward me. Yikes! She looked like she wanted to eat me! The baby seemed excited and started talking. I realized the big gator didn't want to eat me; she was simply the mother coming to get her baby!

Right before my eyes, the big mama picked up the baby in her powerful jaws and swam a short distance away. She released the baby from her mouth, and they swam into the sawgrass and disappeared.

I stood there with my mouth open for a long time. I had never seen reptiles take care of their babies. At that instant, I was hooked. I knew that I wanted to work on crocodilians. I went on to get a PhD working on alligators in the Everglades and I became a herpetologist. A herpetologist is a scientist who works on reptiles and amphibians. After graduating, I went to work for the National Geographic Society as their croc expert. For the last 20 years, I have traveled all over the world researching crocs and learning as much as I can about them so that I can share that information with others. I am the only person that has ever captured all 24 species of croc in the wild. In fact, I am the only person that has ever seen every species in the wild!

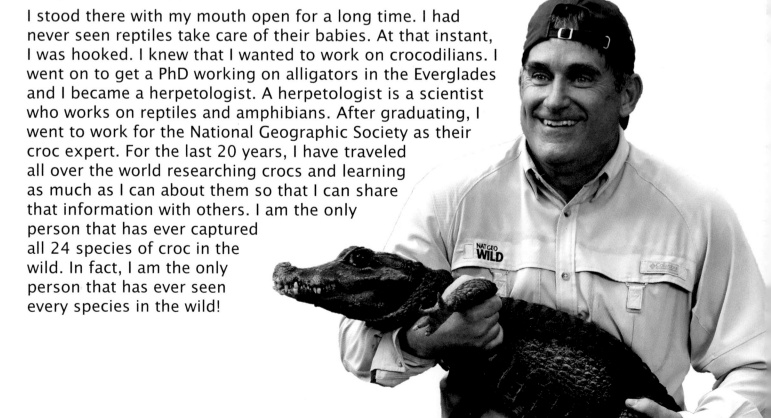

Croc Conservation

Sadly, about a third of all crocs are in big trouble—endangered or threatened with extinction. In fact, crocs are some of the most endangered animals on the planet. Some species have just a handful of individuals left in the wild, like the Siamese Croc, the False Gharial, and the Chinese alligator.

One reason crocs are in trouble is that some humans think it is okay to use croc skins to make shoes, handbags, and belts. Croc skins definitely belong on crocs and nowhere else!

Another reason some crocs are in trouble is that they are losing their habitats, the places they live. In many places, humans are draining wetlands and swamps (places crocs call home) to construct buildings. We humans like waterfront property near beaches, rivers, and lakes. But when we develop these areas, where will the crocs live? When we build on crocs' habitats, we can destroy them and leave crocs homeless.

In addition to destroying habitats, some people kill crocs because they are scared of them, feel that they pose a danger, or even for no reason at all. That isn't right.

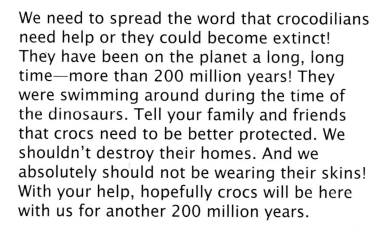

We need to spread the word that crocodilians need help or they could become extinct! They have been on the planet a long, long time—more than 200 million years! They were swimming around during the time of the dinosaurs. Tell your family and friends that crocs need to be better protected. We shouldn't destroy their homes. And we absolutely should not be wearing their skins! With your help, hopefully crocs will be here with us for another 200 million years.

To all the kids and adults in Costa Rica that have taken part in the Crocodile Headstart Program, and helped raise awareness for this amazing and often misunderstood crocodile.—BB
To my mom, Bea Keats.—JKC
For Holli.—SD
Thanks to Jessica Rosnick for her photos of Alexa, and to Mario Aldecoa for his photos on spread 3, 6, 7, 8, 9, and 10.

Thanks to John Brueggen, Director of the St. Augustine Alligator Farm Zoological Park for verifying the accuracy of the information in this book.

Library of Congress Cataloging in Publication Control Number: 2016016123

9781628558340   English hardcover ISBN
9781628558357   English paperback ISBN
9781628558364   Spanish paperback ISBN
9781628558371   English eBook downloadable ISBN
9781628558388   Spanish eBook downloadable ISBN
Interactive, read-aloud eBook featuring selectable English (9781628558395) and Spanish (9781628558401) text and audio (web and iPad/tablet based) ISBN

Translated into Spanish: *Hasta la vista, cocodrilo: El diario de Alexa*

Lexile® Level: NC 770L

keywords: crocodiles, alligators, basic needs, Central America, character, conservation, Costa Rica, environmental education, human interaction, life science, water (river, wetlands)

Bibliography:
"American Crocodile. Crocodylus Acutus." AccessScience (n.d.): n. pag. U.S. Fish and Wildlife Service: American Crocodile. U.S. Fish and Wildlife Service. Web.
Barr, Brady, and Kathleen Weidner Zoehfeld. Crocodile Encounters: And More True Stories of Adventures with Animals. N.p.: National Geographic Children's, 2012. Print.
Britton, Adam. "Crocodilian Biology Database - Integumentary Sense Organs." Crocodilian Biology Database - Integumentary Sense Organs. Crocodilian Biology Database, n.d. Web.
Chenot-Rose, Cherie, and A. Wil. "ACES / American Crocodile Education Sanctuary in Belize, Central America." By: Cherie Chenot-Rose, Biologist/Owner July 5, 2010 (2010): n. pag. American Crocodile Education Sanctuary. Crocodile Education Sanctuary. Web.
"Crocodilians: Natural History and Conservation - Crocodiles, Caimans, Alligators, Gharials." Crocodilians: Natural History and Conservation - Crocodiles, Caimans, Alligators, Gharials. University of Bristol and Florida Museum of Natural History, n.d. Web.
Leff, Alex. "Missing in Costa Rica: Female Crocodiles." Missing in Costa Rica: Female Crocodiles. GlobalPost, 21 Sept. 2010. Web.
Mauger, Laurie A., Elizabeth Velez, Michael Sebastino Cherkiss, Matthew L. Brien, Michael Boston, Frank J. Mazzotti, and James R. Spotila. "Population Assessment of the American Crocodile, Crocodylus Acutus (Crocodilia: Crocodylidae) on the Pacific Coast of Costa Rica." RBT Revista De Biología Tropical 60.4 (2012): n. pag. Population Assessment of the American Crocodile, Crocodylus Acutus (Crocodilia: Crocodylidae) on the Pacific Coast of Costa Rica. Universidad De Costa Rica. Web.

Manufactured in China, May 2016
This product conforms to CPSIA 2008
First Printing

Arbordale Publishing
Mt. Pleasant, SC 29464
www.ArbordalePublishing.com